The Great Escape

"Is she going to be all right?" asked Emily, as the vet emerged from the rescue centre.

"I think so. Beagles are a tough, sturdy breed. She'll need a special diet and vitamins over the next week or so to build up her strength again, but she should pick up quite quickly. It's difficult to tell how long she's been neglected and on the run." The vet paused for a second. "But one thing I can say for sure is that she's got quite a young litter of puppies out there somewhere."

Emily looked at Neil. "Puppies!" they shouted.

Titles in the Puppy Patrol series

1
Teacher's Pet

2
Big Ben

3
Abandoned!

4
Double Trouble

5
Star Paws

6
Tug of Love

7
Saving Skye

8
Tuff's Luck

9
Red Alert

10
The Great Escape

11
Perfect Puppy

More Puppy Patrol stories follow soon

Puppy Patrol
The Great Escape

Jenny Dale

Illustrated by

Mick Reid

A Working Partners Book

MACMILLAN CHILDREN'S BOOKS

Special thanks to Tessa Potter

First published 1998 by Macmillan Children's Books
a division of Macmillan Publishers Limited
25 Eccleston Place, London SW1W 9NF
and Basingstoke

Associated companies throughout the world

Created by Working Partners Limited
London W12 7QY

ISBN 0 330 36938 5

1 3 5 7 9 8 6 4 2

A CIP catalogue record for this book is available from
the British Library.

Typeset in Bookman Old Style by SX Composing DTP, Rayleigh, Essex
Printed and bound in Great Britain by Mackays of Chatham plc, Kent

Chapter One

Neil Parker stopped his bike at the crest of Compton Hill and leant forward on his handlebars. He cracked a wide, beaming smile towards his sister, Emily, as she pulled up alongside him. "Race you back to King Street Kennels. Last one home has to walk bulldog Biffer for the rest of the week."

Emily steadied her bike, looked across at her brother and eyed him suspiciously. "What are you in such a good mood about? I thought Mr Hamley had given you an essay to write yesterday because you made dog noises in his class. You've got no reason to be so cheerful."

"He did – but I don't care! It's the first day of the summer holidays, Em, and we've got six whole weeks to devote to dogs!" Neil and Emily's parents ran a boarding kennels and rescue centre for stray dogs. Everybody in Compton knew about King Street Kennels – or the "Puppy Patrol", as their friends called the Parkers. Neil shouted "C'mon!" and then pushed off down the hill.

As he pedalled furiously to increase his speed, Neil glanced back to see if his sister was catching up. The wind flattened Neil's rough, spiky hair as he put his head down and raced ahead. The turning for the kennels was still about a mile away.

Emily was closing the gap between them.

Neil pedalled faster. Soon he'd be out walking in the woods with Sam, his pet Border collie. And he'd be able to help out around the rescue centre now that he had so much free time on his hands.

"Watch out, Neil!"

Emily's sudden cry shattered his thoughts.

Something streaked across the road in front of him and into the hedgerow.

A moment later there was a screech of tyres and the sound of metal crunching. It happened so quickly, Neil could hardly take it in.

He braked hard. For a second he thought he

was going to shoot over the handlebars, but he miraculously managed to stay in his seat. He put a foot down to steady himself and tried to stop shaking.

Seconds later Emily was beside him. "Did you see that?" she yelled, jumping off her bike.

In front of them on the other side of the road two cars had collided. A large BMW had smashed into the back of a small grey Fiat. The drivers were getting out and didn't seem to be hurt.

Neil noticed that Emily's attention was elsewhere. She wasn't looking at the cars. She was pointing wildly towards the field on their left. "It was a dog! It ran in front of that car. I'm going to see if it's all right."

Emily scrambled down the bank at the roadside. Neil glanced back at the cars. A woman was coming towards him. A man was following her, shouting.

"Did you see what happened?" the woman called out. "Is the dog all right? I don't think I hit it." She was small and fair-haired, wearing jeans and a blue jacket. She looked very concerned.

The man was in his early thirties and was dressed in a dark suit. He was tall and thin with a neat moustache. "Would you come back here!" he yelled after the woman. "Look at the damage you've done to my car! You can't just stop like that without a signal."

The woman turned round calmly. "A dog ran in front of me. I had to stop quickly. You were travelling too close behind. You should have been more careful."

"I was about to overtake you . . ." he stuttered back.

"On this narrow little road? Just calm down. Our insurance companies will sort it out – we'll exchange addresses."

"You've mangled my bumper and cracked the front wing. My headlights are smashed to pieces . . ."

Neil turned away from them. "If everyone is OK I'm going to help my sister find the dog."

The man glared at Neil. "Yes, the dog! The dog's responsible. What are you doing with a dog loose on the main road? I shall want your address, too. I've a good mind to call the police right now." He pulled a mobile phone from his pocket.

Neil's mouth dropped open in disbelief. "But it's not our dog!"

The woman glared at the man. "It wasn't with

4

them. The animal just shot out from the side of the road. Heaven only knows where the poor creature is now." She turned back to Neil. "Come on, I'll help you look."

As they climbed down the bank together, Neil could still hear the man yelling. "Just a minute. Come back! We haven't exchanged addresses yet. I'm late for a meeting."

Neil could see Emily in the far corner of the field. She was kneeling down and keeping very still. Something was lying in front of her on the ground. He suddenly felt his heart racing. Perhaps the dog had been injured after all. He hoped Emily was being careful – they both knew that an injured dog might easily bite if it was in pain. He hurried across the newly cut cornfield. He wanted to call out to Emily but he was worried about frightening the dog. He motioned to the woman behind him to keep as quiet as possible.

As they drew nearer, Neil heard Emily talking softly to the dog. "It's OK, girl. You're all right now."

The dog was trembling but sitting up. Emily was calmly stroking her short, smooth coat. The hound was a beautiful tricoloured beagle, but she looked very grubby. She had a black saddle shape across her back, edged with a soft brown tan. A white diamond stretched from the dog's muzzle to her forehead. The rest of her head was tan but her legs, chest and the end of her tail were a dirty white. She was staring up at Emily with brown, gentle eyes.

"I think she's just frightened," whispered Emily. "I don't think she's hurt. She was running round the field but she stopped when she couldn't get through the hedge. Then she let me come up to her. She's very nervous, though, and look how terribly thin she is."

"Well done, Em." Neil bent down and put out

his hand for the dog to sniff. "Good girl. We'll look after you."

"I hope she doesn't take off again," said Emily, anxiously.

"I think you should stay here while I get help. She obviously trusts you, and we shouldn't risk moving her in case there's something wrong."

The woman knelt down beside them. "Is there anything I can do?" she asked.

Suddenly they heard shouting. The man was at the bottom of the bank near the roadside waving his arms around to attract their attention.

"He'll scare her if he doesn't shut up," hissed Emily.

Neil turned to the woman. "I need to call my dad. We don't live that far away. He'll come and get us."

As they hurried back across the field the woman introduced herself. "I'm Wendy Paget. Is your dad a vet?"

Neil shook his head. "No, we live at King Street Kennels. If I can call my dad he'll know what to do."

"That awful man said something about calling the police. He'll want to report the accident so that he can claim on his insurance.

I'll get him to lend you his mobile phone while we exchange addresses."

Wendy Paget seemed to handle the man very well. He was still angry but he began to calm down as she talked to him.

"This lady tells me your parents run a rescue centre for dogs." The man handed his mobile phone to Neil. "I hope it isn't one of their strays. Make your call and get something done about that dog before it causes another accident."

Neil punched in the number. "Hello, Dad? We need your help." Neil could sense the anxious edge to his father's voice and tried to reassure him that nobody was hurt. He quickly filled him in on the situation and finished, "See you in a couple of minutes."

The man grabbed his phone and jumped into the car. "I've really got to rush – I've got an important meeting. My insurance company will be in touch," he snapped. "Goodbye."

Neil and Wendy watched the car manoeuvre round the other vehicle before speeding away.

"He'll have another accident if he's not careful," said Neil.

Wendy looked at the business card the man had given her. "Well, thanks for your help, Mr P Pritchard of Universal Laboratories, Padsham."

She turned back to Neil. "I'll wait by the road for your dad. You'd better go back and see if your sister's all right."

"Thanks," said Neil. "You'll have no trouble recognizing him. He'll be driving a green Range Rover with King Street Kennels written on the side."

Bob Parker arrived at the scene shortly afterwards and stopped on the grassy roadside verge. He was a large man with thick, dark hair and a sweatshirt emblazoned with the same doggie-logo that was on the vehicle doors.

From the field, Neil heard the car engine and turned round to look back at the road. He saw his father and Mrs Paget up on the bank together. She was pointing in their direction. Moments later Bob Parker was striding across the field towards them.

"Don't scare her, Dad," called Emily, as he approached them. "She's a bit jumpy."

Bob Parker knelt down and gave the dog a quick look-over. He ran his hands along her back and down each leg, checking for signs of injury. The dog was trembling but didn't seem to be in any pain. "She's a beautiful dog underneath all this muck, and she's obviously been cared for in the past, but she's very weak and thin. You say she can walk and run OK?"

Neil and Emily nodded. Bob gently slipped a collar on her and attached a lead to it. "You take her, Emily," he said. "Let's move her back to King Street where we can check her out properly."

Emily stood up stiffly. "Come on, girl."

The beagle responded to Emily's gentle tugs and they walked slowly back towards the road.

"Where do you think she's come from, Dad?" Neil asked. "Judging by the dirt on her paws, she must have been lost for some time. She doesn't have a collar, either. I wonder why somebody didn't want her."

Bob Parker sighed. "I've given up speculating about things like that, Neil. I've known people abandon beautiful, good-tempered pedigree dogs before now for no reason other than they were bored of having them around." He looked down at the dog walking alongside Emily. "Beagles can be difficult to train if you don't know what you're doing. They're very lively."

"Do we need to get her to the vet?" asked Emily.

"Not straight away. Mike Turner's calling round this morning in any case. He's checking up on a couple of the boarders. I think she'll survive until then."

They reached the Range Rover. "Emily, do you want to go in the car with the dog?" said Neil. "I'll follow behind. It might be a bit of a crush with both of our bikes in there."

Emily settled in the back seat of the Range Rover with the dog's white and brown head resting on her lap. "I think she knows we're going to help her," she said, tracing the white diamond on her forehead.

Bob thanked Mrs Paget for her help before getting into the front seat of the car and starting the engine.

Neil tapped on the window. "See you back at the house. I'll be right behind you." He stepped back and stood on the grassy verge with his bike as the car slowly pulled away. Neil was relieved that at least the dog felt secure with someone.

Chapter Two

Neil swerved into the driveway of his home at King Street Kennels and leaned his bike against the parked car. Carole Parker had been waiting outside when Bob and Emily arrived back with the dog. She looked a little anxious, but grinned cheerfully when she saw Neil. A small Pekinese was wriggling under her arm. "Phew! It's all go today!" she said. "I've had two more dogs dropped off while you were out."

Emily gently lifted the beagle down off the back seat of the Range Rover.

"What have you brought us today, then?" asked Carole. "I only sent you out for a card for Kate's birthday." Kate McGuire was the King

Street kennel maid and was almost like one of the family.

Neil explained what had happened as they walked round to the rescue centre. Set a bit further back from the house and main kennel blocks, the rescue centre was a low, square building adjacent to the Parkers' impressive-looking new barn, where Bob Parker held his twice-weekly training classes.

It didn't take Neil and Emily long to settle the beagle into one of the empty pens. The rescue centre was funded by the local council and had room for ten lost or abandoned dogs. Everyone worked tirelessly to help find new owners for them.

Emily knelt beside the beagle, stroking her smooth coat. "I'm sure no one would delib-erately abandon you. Someone must be looking for you, somewhere."

The beagle was lying on a soft blanket in the basket that Emily had put out for her. Her head was resting on her stretched-out paws. She looked up at them but didn't move. A ripple of a sigh seemed to run along her entire body.

Neil placed a metal bowl of water and a small dish of food in front of the dog. "Dad says that we shouldn't overfeed her. We'll leave her to rest for a while. Mike Turner will be here soon to look her over. Come on, Em, she needs some peace."

The beagle began eating hungrily from the dish as Neil and Emily left the rescue centre. They were walking back towards the house when they met Bob coming out of the kennels office shaking his head. "I've been in touch with Sergeant Moorhead and the RSPCA," he said. "There haven't been any missing beagles reported in this area for some time."

"What do you think could have happened to her collar and name tag?" asked Emily, anxiously. "They don't usually just fall off by themselves."

Bob Parker shrugged. "I have no idea. It may have been torn off. Or somebody could have removed it. I've asked Mike to bring his scanner to see if she's got an identification chip."

"Don't worry," said Neil, squeezing his sister's arm gently. "She's going to be all right."

Mike Turner arrived at King Street Kennels in the late afternoon. Neil and Emily rushed out of the house when they heard his car draw up, and were closely followed by five-year-old Sarah – the baby of the family. Sarah ran up to the vet and insisted on helping him with his bag.

Bob Parker emerged from the kennels office and greeted his friend. "Mike. Glad you could make it."

"Sorry, I'm late. There was an emergency at Priorsfield Farm," the vet explained. "One of Harry Grey's sheep got caught up in some wire fencing." He thanked Sarah for her help and ruffled her hair affectionately. "Now, what have you got for me today?"

"How about a basset hound with a grass seed in her ear?" said Bob, smiling.

Mike laughed. "Interesting. Anything else?"

"I'm a bit worried about a Great Dane, too. It's the first time she's boarded with us. She's hardly eating anything and I'd like you to check her out."

"We need you at the rescue centre first, though," said Emily quickly.

Neil and Emily led the way to the beagle's pen. Mike Turner crouched down and peered inside at the frightened dog.

"We found her on the hill a couple of minutes up the road towards Compton," said Emily. "She caused a car accident but I don't think she was injured. Probably more frightened than anything else, but she's so quiet. I'm really worried about her, Mike."

"No one seems to have reported her missing locally, either. We're just hoping she may have been microchipped," added Neil.

"Let's take a proper look at her," said Mike, stepping inside the pen. Emily followed him inside. The beagle licked Emily's outstretched hand, but when the vet came closer, the dog began to back away.

Mike squatted down beside the dog. "Come on, girl, I'm not going to hurt you. You'd better hold her for me, Emily." The beagle was trembling.

"She seems to trust Emily," said Neil, watching through the wire mesh.

Mike Turner took a long time to examine the beagle. He gently felt her for any signs of injury. He listened to her heart and lungs with his stethoscope. Then he used a scanner to check for any signs that a tiny identity chip had been implanted in the rough folds of skin at the back of her neck. At last, the vet stood up. "We'll leave her now. She needs to sleep."

Outside the rescue centre, Mike shook his head. "No luck with the scanner, I'm afraid. Her identity is still a mystery. That distinctive diamond shape on her head should help when you describe her to people though. She's very weak and dehydrated but I can't see anything more serious."

"Is she going to be all right?" asked Emily, anxiously.

"I think so. Beagles are a tough, sturdy breed. They've been bred for hunting hares and have a lot of stamina. She'll need a special diet and vitamins over the next week or so to build up her strength again, but she should pick up quite quickly. It's difficult to tell how long she's been neglected and on the run." The vet paused for a second. "But one thing I can say for sure is that she's got quite a young litter of puppies out there somewhere."

"Puppies!" said Neil and Emily together.

"Yes, and I hate to think what kind of state they may be in. She only stopped feeding them very recently. Her milk hasn't properly dried up yet. Underneath the dirt I found that her teats are still a little enlarged. I shouldn't think the pups are much more than six or seven weeks old."

"Hardly old enough to be without their mother," said Emily, quietly. "We should go and look for them. They might be wandering about in the fields near to where we found her."

"Possibly. They may well be in need of my attention." The vet began to scribble in a notebook. "The mother here will certainly be a beautiful dog when she's in good condition again."

"I bet she has a decent pedigree. She looks pure-bred. Best beagle I've seen for ages. Her puppies are probably quite valuable," said Bob.

"Emily and I will go out and scout round for them," said Neil. "We've got to find them."

Mike nodded. "I think you're right. Now, Bob, where are those other dogs you've got for me?"

Bob and Mike walked off towards the kennel blocks.

Kate McGuire called out to Neil and Emily as

they were heading across the courtyard towards the house. Long strands of blonde hair had escaped from her ponytail and she was looking a bit frazzled. Four eager dogs were straining at their leads, impatient for their walk. "Neil! Emily! I'm just taking these four out for some exercise."

"Great," said Neil. "Sam could do with a run. And we need to go out anyway."

"We're on a mission," said Emily, seriously.

"What do you mean?" asked Kate.

Neil leant inside the kitchen and unhooked Sam's lead from behind the door. "Can we take a different route, Kate? We need to find a litter of beagle pups who've lost their mum."

A few minutes later they were in open fields, heading towards the hill where Neil and Emily had found the beagle mother. The sun was burning down and they were grateful for the light breeze that helped keep them cool. Neil grinned as he watched Sam bounding backwards and forwards along the path that ran adjacent to the road. The sheepdog's sleek black and white coat shone in the sunlight and his wet black nose quivered at every new smell. He, at least, was in peak condition.

"Here, boy!" Neil called. Sam darted forward to his side, wagging his tail ecstatically as Neil ruffled his ears. He could feel the dog trembling with anticipation. Sam's bright, intelligent eyes stared up at him – waiting intently for Neil's next instruction, waiting to be released to continue his run. "OK, boy! Off you go!"

Sam shot away like an arrow.

"This is it," said Emily, as they climbed over a stile which brought them into the cornfield they had been in that morning.

Neil scanned the field. "There's not much cover, is there? Where could the pups be hiding

– if they're even still round here?"

Kate glanced round. "Let's try looking along the hedgerows and in the field across the road too."

After what seemed like ages searching under every bush, tree and thorny hedgerow, Emily wiped her brow, flopped down into some long grass and sighed. "Nothing. Absolutely nothing."

Neil shrugged and kicked at a chunk of mud on the ground. "We tried our best, Emily. We had to be sure they weren't here."

"Then where are they?"

Kate sat down on a tree stump and patted one of the dogs panting near her feet, a hairy, grey miniature schnauzer. "Come on, you two. Don't get too upset about it. I'm sure you'll think of some other way of tracking them down." Kate smiled. "You always do. Let's go up to the ridgeway and give the dogs a proper run before we head back."

Neil and Emily picked themselves up and dusted themselves down. "OK."

"Thank goodness we're nearly at the top," Kate puffed, as she climbed the final few metres towards the top of the Compton Vale ridgeway.

"Is it just me or does this hill get steeper every time?"

"It's the heat," said Neil. "I only hope it stays like this for the rest of the holidays."

On top of the ridge, Neil turned round a few times and admired the view. In the distance he could see Compton. He picked out his school, Meadowbank Primary, and the tall spire of the parish church.

Emily pointed out the field where they had just been looking for the pups. "It's a good job we found their mother when we did. I don't know how much longer she'd have lasted in this heat without water."

Kate nodded and sat down on a huge rock to get her breath back. "It'll be tough on the puppies, too. I hope they're getting regular drinks. I wonder what can have happened to them?"

"Surely no one would *dump* a litter of puppies," pondered Neil, rubbing his aching feet. "Although I've never heard of anyone *losing* a whole litter of puppies, either. I suppose they could still be with the owners."

"Yes, but if the owners have got the puppies," said Emily, "why aren't they searching for the mother? It just doesn't make sense. I'm sure the puppies are somehow the key to it all."

"Neither of you can remember anything about lost beagle pups in the Compton News, then?" asked Kate, placing the handle loops of her dog leads over her foot. She didn't want any of the dogs to run away.

Emily frowned and thought hard. "Not me." The Parkers checked the lost and found column in the *Compton News* every week.

"Me neither," said Neil, scratching his chin. "Nothing specifically about missing puppies, anyway." Suddenly his face lit up. "Hang on. I'm sure I remember a news item, though. I think it was something about a *pregnant* dog that had gone missing. A dog *about* to have puppies!" He stood up excitedly. "We've got to get back. I've got to look it up. It might be the same dog!" Neil ran headlong down the hill with Sam barking excitedly at his heels. Kate and Emily followed him and tried to keep up.

"Neil, what are you talking about?" asked Emily, breathlessly.

"Don't you remember? A woman had contacted loads of local papers all over the region because she was so desperate to find her missing dog."

"And the dog was definitely about to have

puppies?" queried Kate, running alongside Neil. Her four dogs were thoroughly enjoying this renewed burst of energy at the end of their long walk.

"Yes. That's what made it stick out in my mind. It might even have been a beagle. We could have solved this already!"

24

Chapter Three

Neil rushed through the back door at King Street Kennels, and hastily filled up Sam's bowl with water, sloshing it all over the kitchen doorstep. "Whoops! Sorry, Sam! Got to dash." The collie lapped it up thirstily, ignoring Neil's strange behaviour. Neil charged into the kitchen and immediately bumped into Sarah and his mum who were on their way out.

"Watch out!" said Carole. "What's your hurry?"

"Newspapers!" Neil bounced round the kitchen grabbing every paper he could lay his hands on. He took some from a pile under the sink and others from a box in the cupboard.

Soon he had a huge, unsteady pile in his arms.

"Those are Fudge's!" shrieked Sarah. Neil's sister was very attached to her pet hamster and hated to think that her big brother was taking away his future bedding.

"Fudge can have them back as soon as I've looked through them – and he'd better not have had the one I want," snapped Neil.

"Neil's being nasty," wailed Sarah.

"Not really, sweetheart," said Carole. "I think he's just looking for something. There are some more papers under the stairs, Neil."

"Cheers!"

When they had gone, Neil dumped his papers in a space on the kitchen table.

Emily sat beside him and grabbed a paper off the pile. "What exactly are we looking for?"

"A news feature about a missing dog from up north somewhere. Was it Middlesbrough?"

"But Neil, that's over a hundred miles away. It can't be the dog we found."

"From what I remember, the owner couldn't find it locally. She'd tried everything," said Neil excitedly. "That's why she'd widened the search."

"Well, let's sort these papers out first. How long ago exactly was it?"

Neil shrugged. "I'm not sure. A month. Maybe two. I think it was before half-term."

"There are hardly any that far back, anyway. We won't bother with anything before May. Chuck those in a pile on the floor. Then we'll start reading. Was there a picture of the dog?"

"I think so," said Neil, opening the first paper and beginning to scan the pages.

Neil and Emily were still reading when Carole Parker and Sarah returned home an hour later. Neil was looking very dejected. "It's no good," he said. "It's not here. There are loads of issues missing. Sarah must have used it for her stupid hamster. I really thought we were on to something."

"Come on, Neil," said his mum. "That's unfair. It's not Sarah's fault. She's *supposed* to use the old papers."

Sarah was looking quite upset.

"Sorry," Neil mumbled.

"What's this all about, anyway?" Carole Parker asked.

Neil told her about the article. His mum shook her head. "It seems a bit of a long shot to me. Middlesbrough is so far away. Why would the dog have strayed here? In any case, if it was that long ago, she'll probably have turned up by now."

"The dog might have been stolen. It could be anywhere by now. There's no reason why it can't be the one we've found."

"Have a look at the clippings file in the office, too," said Carole. "I can't remember anything about a beagle, or beagle pups, but you never know."

Neil shook his head. "But I'm convinced I remember a *news* story, not a mention in the lost and found column."

"We should look in the back copies of the paper in the library, then," suggested Emily.

Neil brightened. "Good idea, Em. Let's go." Neil got up and scraped his chair along the wooden kitchen floor.

"Neil, it's Saturday afternoon – the library will be closed."

Neil sat back down again. There was nothing more he could do.

"Is it always this hectic in July?" groaned Carole Parker. "I can't remember a Saturday as busy as this for ages." Everyone was sitting in the kitchen taking a well-earned rest.

"Yep," grinned Bob and Kate together.

"And there are still two new arrivals to come," said Carole, taking a sip from her cup of steaming coffee.

"It's not usually this hot though," said Emily, wiping her forehead dramatically.

"I've felt really sticky all day," added Neil.

"Fudge is sweating too," said Sarah, slurping her lemonade noisily.

"Hamsters don't sweat, silly," scolded Neil.

"I'd keep checking that his water bottle's full, if I were you," said Bob Parker.

"How's the beagle doing?" asked Carole.

"She was asleep when I last looked in," said Neil. "Mike says that she needs all the rest she can get after what she's been through."

"She certainly hasn't been getting the right kind of food. I don't think she'd eaten at all for a few days," said Bob.

Emily sighed. "Someone must be really worried about her. I hope her puppies are managing to fend for themselves."

"I'm afraid we won't know until we find them," replied Bob. "But at least lots of people are on the lookout for them, and it's not easy to hide a whole litter of hungry pups."

"I'm sure she's the dog from that article,"

insisted Neil. "If only we could make a wider appeal for information about her. You know, Dad, if only we had a modem and scanner for the computer . . ." He glanced at his father sheepishly.

"Not that one again!" laughed Bob Parker.

"No, seriously, Dad. If we created our own King Street Kennels website, we would be able to scan in pictures of any lost dogs that we found. People looking for a dog anywhere in England would be able to visit our website to see if we had found it."

"From anywhere in the world," added Emily.

"It would help advertise the business too," Neil persisted. "Really, Dad. More and more people are getting access to the Internet. There's even a Select-a-dog site, a database to help match people to the right kind of pet. You answer questions like how experienced you are, how big your garden is and how much exercise you would be able to give a dog."

Bob Parker nodded. "Well, I'm all for that. The rescue centre might not be so busy if people didn't take on the wrong kind of dog in the first place."

"So does that mean we can have one then?" asked Neil.

"No."

Carole smiled. "It sounds a great idea, Neil. I'm sure there are lots of practical uses we could put it to. But there just isn't any money around for it at the moment."

Neil pulled a face.

Emily looked out of the window dreamily. "It would be brilliant. There are loads of wildlife sites I could visit. And chat rooms where you can talk to other people who love dogs. We could get campaigns and petitions organized, and send e-mail . . ."

Sam poked his snout out from underneath the table and barked, as if in agreement.

"You see, even Sam thinks it's a good idea!" laughed Neil.

"Steady on! I don't know about you, Carole, but I feel we're being ganged up on here!" Bob chuckled.

Carole Parker sat back in her chair. "The fact is, we can't afford it. Rebuilding the barn after the fire this year was terribly expensive, even though the insurance money paid for most of it."

"It's just that we want to help the rescue centre dogs as much as possible," said Emily.

"And we *really* want to find the beagle puppies," added Neil.

"I know," Carole said, sympathetically. "Look, why don't you go over to the exercise field and fill up Sarah's old paddling pool for Sam. He'll enjoy a splash in that and it might help you cool down, too."

"Good idea," said Neil.

Sarah jumped up. "And me! Please, Neil, please let me!"

Neil looked at Emily and groaned. It was going to be a long night.

On Sunday morning, a loud chorus of barking signalled the early arrival of Kate McGuire. Neil was lying awake in his bed. He felt like rolling over and trying to go back to sleep, but his thoughts kept turning to the lost dog in the rescue centre. Where had she come from? If only he could find the beagle's owner and locate her missing puppies. Monday, his next opportunity to look through some more newspapers, seemed so far away.

An urgent knocking on the front door of the house interrupted his thoughts. Neil heard his dad stumbling down the stairs, then Kate's voice. She sounded worried.

"Sorry, Bob, I thought I should wake you. There's something here you ought to see."

Neil leapt out of bed, scrambled into some clothes and pelted downstairs. Something was going on that he didn't want to miss.

"What is it, Kate?" came Bob's bleary voice. "What's the problem?"

"Come and see." Kate beckoned Bob outside and Neil slipped into the fresh morning air before the door was closed behind them.

Kate was standing beside the main gatepost at the entrance to the drive. Tied to it was a whimpering cocker spaniel puppy. Its owner was nowhere in sight.

Chapter Four

Kate untied the dog and gently lifted it up into her arms. Almost at once, the dog stopped making a noise. "I spotted him as soon as I arrived. I don't think he's been there long." The puppy's dark, sorrowful eyes were looking up at her. His black and white flecked coat was badly matted. Kate stroked his long silky ears. "There's a good boy. Don't be scared," she cooed.

"He's a blue roan, isn't he?" Neil whispered. "He's fantastic." The dog's mixture of black and white hairs shone a mottled grey colour in the early light. A white star of fur twinkled on the top of his smooth black head.

Bob Parker coughed. "We'd better get him

inside. He must only be about six months old." He held out his hand for the puppy to sniff. "I bet you can be a bit of a rascal, can't you? Was he left with a note or anything, Kate?"

Kate shook her head. "There wasn't anything tied to the gate."

"Look, Dad," said Neil. "There's something attached to his collar."

"Put him down, Kate, and we'll have a look."

Kate held the puppy's lead while Neil tried to unravel a small twisted plastic bag from his collar. Once he was on the floor, the puppy wouldn't keep still. He seemed more intent on scrambling over Neil's shoes and jumping up to lick his face than allowing him to inspect his collar. "Hey! Keep still. Ouch!" Neil yelled as the young dog playfully nipped his fingers. At last, he managed to detach the bag and tore it open. A handful of coins clattered onto the floor.

"They must have left this money for his food," said Kate.

Bob Parker shrugged. "It won't go very far."

"At least they've tried to do something right, Dad," said Neil. "This must be better than just dumping him on the motorway."

"True. You're right, Neil. I just wish people would consider the consequences before taking on a puppy. The trouble with cockers is that they look absolutely adorable, and they are extremely affectionate – but they're often quite highly strung and excitable, too. They have a lot of energy and can be a real handful."

"As we've just found out," said Neil.

After breakfast, Neil and Emily watched the cocker spaniel through the wire mesh of his new home in the rescue centre. The puppy rattled round his pen, eagerly pouncing on a rubber ball and squeaky bone. Then he stopped running and sat looking round, as if he was slightly puzzled.

"What's he got in his mouth?" asked Emily, tilting her head to one side to try and make out what the object was.

Neil chuckled. "It's one of Dad's slippers. He grabbed it when we were walking him over here earlier this morning. Time to retrieve it, I think."

"How are going to do that? He looks fairly attached to it."

Neil grinned. "Watch." He opened the door of the pen and stepped inside. Kneeling down, he fished out a small doggie treat from his pocket and held it between his fingers in his outstretched hand. "Here, boy."

The pup immediately dropped the slipper and dived for the treat. "Thank you!" said Neil triumphantly. He grabbed the slipper and Emily starting clapping. Having wolfed down the treat, the puppy looked round for the missing slipper.

"I'm impressed," said Emily. "But what would you have done if the puppy hadn't been hungry?"

"I've never known a cocker spaniel that wasn't! I suspect he's been grabbing and chewing everything he could get his paws on since he was born. C'mon, let's go and see Kate. She'll be getting the feeds ready and we can help with the beagle."

They found Kate measuring out dog food for

the boarders. She knew the requirements for the regulars, but a couple of new dogs were on diets she hadn't prepared before. The dogs were always fed whatever they were used to at home.

"Hi! Do you think you could see to Ben for me?" Kate looked up from her clipboard. "Here's his bowl. Julie has told you what he eats, hasn't she? He needs some water too."

"Sure," said Emily, grabbing scoops of dog food from one of the different bags and tins. "No problem." Ben was a big, shaggy Old English sheepdog that belonged to one of Emily's best friends from school. Julie had gone on holiday to Scotland and Emily had promised to take extra-special care of him.

"I'll take the beagle's," volunteered Neil.

"Great," said Kate. "You can make up her food yourself. Mike Turner's left her some special supplements. I've got the instructions here. She's got to have four small meals a day to build up her strength."

Neil clutched his dishes of food and water then walked quickly across to the rescue centre. Most of the dogs knew it was feeding time and were making a lot of noise as he approached. "Shut up, will you!" he yelled jokily as he kicked open the main door with his foot.

The beagle was curled up in her basket. Her tan head, topped with its long rounded ears and white diamond, was resting on her paws. Her eyes were open and she looked up at Neil as he quietly opened the pen.

Emily joined him after feeding Ben and knelt down by the dog's basket. She gently began to stroke her ears. "We've brought you some food," she whispered. The beagle's eyes had a sad, pleading expression and Emily would have given anything to see just one wag of her white-tipped tail, but she didn't move.

"I've put the food down here, Em. Let's leave her and see what she does."

They waited quietly outside the pen. Slowly the beagle uncurled and stretched herself. She climbed out of the basket and walked unsteadily towards the food. Then she began to eat, hesitantly at first, but then with increasing assurance. A couple of minutes later, the bowl was empty. She moved to her water and began to drink. She paused and looked up at them.

"Good girl!" whispered Emily, encouragingly.

Neil thought he saw the faintest hint of a tail wag as the beagle put her head down again and continued drinking.

When she had finished, the beagle began to

pace round the pen, sniffing the ground where Neil and Emily had walked. Then she seemed to lose interest. She climbed into her basket and curled up tightly.

"Do you think she misses her puppies?" asked Emily as they walked back to the house.

"I don't know. Puppies aren't usually fully weaned until seven or eight weeks, and even then they still spend some time with their mother." Neil sighed. "I just wish we could find out what's happened to them."

The highlight of Sunday afternoon for Sarah was helping to wash and trim the young spaniel puppy abandoned at the Parkers' front gate. The highlight for Neil was *watching* Sarah help wash and trim the spaniel – he knew it was going to be messy and very funny.

Neil sat the puppy on the treatment table in the kennels store. All the grooming equipment was kept here. There was a bath and grooming table and a special drying cabinet, which they used in the winter.

Sarah had wanted to help Kate on her own but another pair of more experienced hands was definitely necessary. "I'll have to hold him for Kate," Neil told her. "But you can help rub in the shampoo. We don't know yet whether he likes having baths."

The puppy loved the water. "He looks like a little otter!" Sarah giggled, peering into the dog bath to rub noses with him. The puppy leapt up towards her, scrabbling at the sides of the bath.

"He looks more like a drowned rabbit with long droopy ears," said Neil.

Once or twice the squirming puppy slipped from Sarah's gentle grasp and splashed everybody with waves of soapy water. Neil finally caught and covered the puppy with a large towel. Sarah helped rub him dry after his bath and Kate helped to dry Sarah. Neil wiped down the table and other surfaces that had got wet in the process.

Kate ran her fingers through the tangled black and grey puppy fur – the long hair on his legs and chest and tummy was completely matted.

"How are we going to get those tangles out?" asked Neil.

Kate shook her head. "We can't. The conditioner I've used hasn't made any difference. He should have been groomed every day to keep his feathers free of knots." She tugged on the bits of long hair on the puppy's legs and tummy. "I'll have to shave them off with the electric clippers."

"You can't shave him!" protested Sarah. "I don't want him to be bald!"

"He won't be bald," said Kate, reaching for the electric clippers hung up on a hook on the wall. "And his hair will soon grow long again. If you help me brush him every day, we'll manage to keep him free of tangles. The noise may frighten him a bit so we'll have to work very slowly to start with. Here, Sarah," she said, handing her some dog treats. "I want you to be ready with these."

Neil held the little spaniel while Kate switched on the clippers. The black and white puppy jumped nervously at the noise. Kate nodded to Sarah. "OK, give him one of the treats."

While the puppy munched the treat, Kate gently began to shave one leg. Then she told Sarah to give him another. "There's a good boy!" said Kate moving onto the puppy's next leg. "This way the puppy learns that it really isn't too bad, being clipped."

When Kate had finished, the table was covered with piles of matted fur. Neil lifted the pup gently down to the floor. He scampered away, shaking himself, pleased to be free.

"He'll feel better in this heat without that thick coat," said Neil, admiring their handi-work. They watched as the little shorn puppy tore round the room. His legs looked very thin and spindly and his body looked like a smooth round barrel.

Sarah laughed. "Look at him! He looks just like a little black lamb! Can we call him Baa?"

Neil and Kate exchanged glances but both ended up smiling. "OK. Baa it is," agreed Neil. It was usual to give names to all the unclaimed dogs in the rescue centre and Neil suddenly found himself thinking about the beagle again. They hadn't given her a name yet. Somehow it hadn't felt right. She still had a name of her own. He was sure that somewhere, someone was thinking about her, still using that name, hoping that they would one day find her.

Through the window, they saw a grey Fiat drive up. Neil looked at the car and thought it appeared familiar. Kate suddenly started and looked at her watch. "Is that the time already? I shall have to dash, Neil – a friend's come to collect me. Can you and Sarah take Baa back to the rescue centre?"

"Sure."

Neil stepped outside and watched Kate run up and greet the young man who got out of the car. He was tall and well-built, with a baggy white T-shirt. His blond hair was long and swept back. Neil guessed that he was a couple of years older than Kate. She waved at Neil to come over. Glancing over his shoulder to check that Sarah and Baa were happily inside the storeroom playing together, he went over to join them.

"Neil, this is Glen," said Kate, introducing the man. He cracked a wide smile and shook Neil's hand.

"Pleased to meet you, Neil. Kate reckons you know as much as she does about dogs. Almost!"

Neil laughed. "I taught her everything she knows, Glen!"

"I'll leave my bike here today, Neil. Glen can give me a lift back tomorrow."

Bob Parker emerged from the office. "Hope the meeting goes well. Fill me in on what happens when I see you next."

Glen nodded his head. "Great, I'd be glad to." He jumped into the car and closed the door. Kate waved from the passenger seat as they drove off.

"What meeting? Where are they going to, Dad?" Neil asked.

"Glen's a student at Padsham Agricultural College. Apparently there's some concern that Universal Laboratories, the new research centre on the main road outside Padsham, may be testing cosmetics on animals. Glen belongs to an animal protection group who've got some inside information on it."

"Who was that?" asked Emily, appearing beside them. "He looked a bit dishy!"

"Kate's new boyfriend," said Neil, matter-of-factly. "He says the new research centre is using animals to test make-up."

"Steady on, Neil," said Bob Parker. "He said they *might* be using animals. We know nothing for certain yet. And we don't know that he's actually Kate's boyfriend!"

Neil nudged his sister in the ribs. "Dad, get real! Of course he is. You should have seen her jump when his car arrived."

"Well, regardless, do you remember Mrs Paget?" said Bob. "She was the woman who stopped to help you with the beagle yesterday. She's Glen's mum."

"I thought the car looked familiar. She had that damage sorted out pretty quickly."

Emily was hardly listening. She was re-membering a television documentary she had seen recently where a laboratory had been infiltrated and exposed for its ill-treatment of animals. She could see the pictures now – rows and rows of cages. Dogs in cages. *Beagles* in cages. Beagles staring forlornly through iron bars; beagles with terrible sores on their backs, tubes being forced down their throats . . . It was all so horrible and cruel. And now a research centre had opened just a few miles away, where they might be using animals, too.

Bob Parker looked at his watch and mumbled something about having to get back to work. He turned round and headed back towards the kennels office.

Emily remained rooted to the spot. She turned to her brother with an ashen face. "Neil," she said, quietly, "I think our lost beagle might have come from that place. She might have escaped from the new research centre."

Neil stared at her and immediately under-stood what she was saying. "Do you think Universal Laboratories took the beagle to test make-up on her puppies?"

"It can't just be a coincidence. The puppies may still be there. We've got to get over there."

Neil frowned. "It's possible, I suppose. But what can we do?"

"I've got to see the place for myself. Can you imagine what they may be doing to those puppies right now?" Emily turned and ran to get her bike.

Neil stared after her anxiously. If there was a chance that the puppies were still alive, he had to help her. "Wait!" he called out. "I'm coming with you."

Chapter Five

The Universal Laboratories research centre was on the outskirts of Padsham town centre. Neil and Emily had pedalled along the busy main road from Compton, full of hordes of slow-moving cars and caravans, and arrived exhausted outside. Set well back from the road, the large site on which the research centre stood had been tastefully landscaped. Large mounds of earth were piled up to obscure the twisting complex of low buildings. A white noticeboard, surrounded by a selection of bright bedding plants, was planted at the beginning of the short driveway.

"*Universal Laboratories*," Emily read out

loud. *"No unauthorized entry. All visitors to report to reception."*

"This is it, then," said Neil.

They leaned their bikes against some of the young trees that had been planted in front of a tall perimeter fence. In a few years the buildings wouldn't be noticeable at all from the road.

"It looks like a prison," whispered Emily breathlessly, looking up at the impenetrable barrier in front of them. The vast expanse of metal fencing was crowned by twists of menacing barbed wire.

Neil grabbed his bike again. "Come on, let's take a closer look."

Slowly they began to push their bikes up the drive towards the main gate. The white sentry-like box and road barrier were unmanned but the huge gates beyond were firmly closed.

"I guess they're not so busy on a Sunday. There's no one here. We can't possibly get in," said Emily.

Neil pointed to the surveillance cameras mounted high on the fence. "They haven't skimped on the security. They must have something to hide."

Suddenly a slow whirring noise caught their attention. The nearest camera sprang to life and pivoted slowly towards them. Neil and Emily stood still for a moment and there was a strange silence. Their hearts thumped in time to a red light flashing on the side of the camera.

"I don't like this," whispered Emily, trying not to move her lips.

Neil was less cautious. "Ssh!" he signalled. His face had gone white. "Listen!"

Straining their ears, Neil and Emily detected a sound. Barely audible, and very faint, it was coming from somewhere on the other side of the fence inside the complex. A low whining grew louder and more persistent.

Neil gripped the fence and strained to see. "Emily, they have got dogs in there! I told you!"

As the whining gave way to a sudden angry bark, Emily vigorously pulled at Neil's sleeve. "Let's get out of here. There's nothing we can do."

Neil looked round but still couldn't see where the noise was coming from. He reluctantly loosened his grip and allowed Emily to pull him away.

They scrambled onto their bikes and rejoined the passing holiday traffic.

Half an hour later, clutching cold drinks and flapping their T-shirts, Neil and Emily were sitting in the kitchen at King Street Kennels. "Why would Universal Laboratories have all that security?" said Neil, gulping back his third glass of water. "I'm sure something's going on in there. How are we going to get the puppies out?"

"We're still not sure they're in there, Neil. We heard barking, not little puppy yaps."

"Perhaps Kate and Glen will be able to tell us more tomorrow, after their meeting," said Emily.

Their conversation was interrupted by the arrival of Sarah. She burst through the kitchen door crying and dramatically flung herself across the kitchen table between them. Carole Parker followed her inside.

"They're going to take Baa away," Sarah wailed.

"Oh, come on, Sarah," said Carole. "Those people haven't come especially for *him*. They might choose *any* dog. You know your father won't let a dog go to a home unless he feels it's right."

"But Baa's so sweet, they'll want him and *I* love him," she cried.

Carole Parker glanced at Neil and Emily. They seemed uninterested in Sarah's emotional antics. "What's the matter with you two?" she asked.

"We've been over to the new research centre in Padsham," said Emily. "We think they might have the beagle puppies."

"Really?" replied Carole, sounding slightly astonished. "You've been all the way over there?"

"It's like a prison. It's awful," Neil blurted out. "We definitely heard dogs barking. You've heard what they do. They put chemicals into rabbits' eyes to see if they go blind, they shut dogs up in small cages and force them to eat poison, they do terrible things to mice and rats . . ."

"Neil!" said his mother sharply, nodding towards Sarah as a fresh round of wailing broke out from the table. She was wide-eyed and had been listening to every word.

"I won't let them hurt Fudge!" cried Sarah.

"Don't worry, Squirt," Emily said, rubbing her sister's shoulder. "No one's going to touch Fudge."

"I've read that a lot of animals do get stolen for research," said Neil. "If they stole the beagle for her puppies then we've got to rescue them."

"Bob!" cried Carole as her husband walked through the door. "Can you help me out here?"

Sarah picked herself up and ran to Bob, clutching at his legs and sobbing. "I don't want Baa to go to a new home yet!"

Bob Parker lifted her up. "Baa's not ready to go away yet, and he's not really suitable for that family. They've never had a dog before and the woman quite liked the thought of taking the collie cross who came in last week. She's a lot older and has already been trained." He turned to Neil. "They're coming back next week. Perhaps you could take her out into the exercise field with them when they do, Neil. Neil?"

Neil was staring at the kitchen table.

Carole sighed and looked across at Bob. "It's

this research centre. They're getting a bit worked up about it."

Bob sat down at the table. "Come on, guys, we haven't really got any facts yet. We don't know for sure that animals are being used for testing cosmetics. If it does turn out that they are, then we'll do all we can to help Glen with his campaign. There's no justification for any animal being made to suffer so that people can make themselves look beautiful."

"But we have to help the beagle puppies *now*," insisted Neil. "We have no idea what has already been done to them."

"I can't believe they really have those puppies, Neil," said Bob. "I'm not even sure that dogs are used for cosmetic testing any more. Give it a rest, eh? We're doing all we can to help the beagle. We've alerted all the agencies about her and the puppies, and you're going to check out that article in the library tomorrow. I'm sure something's going to come up soon."

Neil got up and pushed his chair away. "Well, there must be something I can do."

"Where are you going?" asked Emily anxiously.

"To check those newspapers again. Anything's better than sitting round here and doing nothing." Neil picked up his drink and marched out of the room.

Emily smiled at her dad sheepishly and then followed him.

Chapter Six

The next day, Neil and Emily were up early. They wanted to spend some more time with the beagle before the library opened and to make sure her recovery was going according to plan.

The beagle greeted them with a slow wag of her tail when they opened her door in the rescue centre. She sat down at Emily's feet and lifted one paw.

"Neil! Look! I think she's getting used to us," said Emily, crouching down and gently shaking the paw.

"She's showing us what she can do. You're a clever girl, aren't you?"

The beagle nestled up against Emily. She

rested her head on Emily's knee and then tried to sniff and lick Neil's hand when he stroked her long silky ears. This time, she didn't back away. "I think she knows we're trying to help her," said Neil. "She likes us. She's getting her strength back – just as Mike predicted."

"She's beautiful, too," said Emily, smiling. "When she's fully recovered and back with her pups she'll be even better."

Neil looked at his watch. "C'mon. Breakfast first, then we'll head off into town. We've got to find that article." He stroked the beagle again. "For her sake."

Neil and Emily sat waiting on the steps of Compton Library fifteen minutes before opening time. The beagle had been in and out of Neil's thoughts since Saturday. "We've been through the other papers at home twice now and there's definitely nothing in them about the beagle," said Neil wearily.

"You start on the ones we haven't read and I'll see what books they've got on cosmetic testing," said Emily. "I want to find the rules and regulations about what you can test on different animals."

After what seemed like an age, the heavy

wooden doors of the library creaked open and a wiry-looking librarian beckoned them in. Once inside they separated and Neil headed towards the local reference section where back issues of the *Compton News* were kept. When he found the file he wanted, he took it and sat at a large oak table near the shelving. He began to read the first newspaper, scanning and turning each page as quickly as he could.

Ten minutes later a whoop of delight from Neil brought Emily running in from the next room. "I've got it, Em!" he cried.

The librarian behind the front desk peered at them disapprovingly.

"Sorry," whispered Neil. He turned to Emily, pointed at the open newspaper spread in front of him and tried to talk more quietly. "The article's so small I nearly missed it. There's no picture, either. It's dated the beginning of June. I reckon that's about right."

Emily peered over his shoulder. "What does it say?"

"Listen to this. The article's headed *Missing from Middlesbrough . . . In a desperate hunt for her missing dog, widow Mrs Joan Thompson has contacted more than one hundred provincial papers across the north and north-west regions.*

Bella, her daughter's four-year-old champion beagle, went missing from Stewart's Park near her home fourteen days ago. All attempts to find Bella in her local area have failed. Concern is growing because Bella is due to have puppies within the next couple of days. 'We're deva-stated,' said Mrs Thompson, 42, of Ayresome Park Road. 'Bella belongs to my nine-year-old daughter, Sally. The dog was my husband's last present to her before he died.'"

"That's awful," said Emily. "Sally's my age. She must be so upset. Wouldn't it be wonderful if we really had found her dog?" Emily paused. "But if it is Bella, how could she have got all the way down here?"

Neil looked at Emily. "She was stolen by the research centre, of course." He began scanning the page again. "There's no phone number here. How are we going to get in touch with the owner? And I'm sure I remember a picture of a dog."

"Jake might be able to help us out," suggested Emily. Neil and Emily often asked the friendly local photographer at the *Compton News* to feature dogs in need from the rescue centre in the newspaper. "He might know something that could tell us more."

59

Neil shook his head. "No, he's on holiday. Three weeks in France. I remember him saying he wouldn't be back until next week."

"Oh. Perhaps there's another article later on, then. C'mon, we'll both look," said Emily, grabbing some of the papers.

Half an hour later, Neil and Emily had completed their search and not found any further mentions of Bella, the missing beagle. They were both feeling very dejected.

"We can't go through them again," said Neil. "We've read them from cover to cover already."

"And I didn't find any books on cosmetics testing, either," said Emily. "What are we going to do now?"

"No luck?" asked the librarian, who was stacking some nearby shelves. "If you're searching for something local, are you sure it was the *Compton News*? Have you tried the *Advertiser*?"

"The *Advertiser!*" yelled Neil, jumping up.

"Sh!" said Emily and the librarian together.

Neil didn't move. "What's the *Advertiser*?" he whispered.

"You know," said Emily. "That thin free paper

which gets shoved through our door every fortnight – if they remember to deliver it. It's mostly advertisements but there are some news stories in there."

"I'll get them for you." The librarian disappeared and came back a moment later with another pile of newspapers. "Try these," she said.

This time Emily nearly jumped out of her seat. She found what she was looking for in the first paper she picked up. "Look! Bella! There's a picture! It *is* her. The markings are the same. She has a diamond on her forehead! And see how that white bit on her chest comes round the left side of her neck."

"Let me see!" Neil could hardly contain himself. "*Reward offered for Missing Mum,*" Neil began. "*Owners lose hope for Bella the missing beagle . . . After six weeks on the run, hopes are fading for Bella and her newborn pups. Her owner has made a dramatic TV appeal for her return.*"

"Is there a phone number?" asked Emily.

Neil scanned the rest of the article and nodded. "Yes, there is. Let's get this photo-copied and get home. Have you got any change for the machine?"

While Neil was photocopying the article, the librarian came over to Emily with some leaflets. "I'm sorry we didn't have any books on what you wanted. Would these be any good to you instead?" she asked. "We had quite a few copies left here the other day. There's a lot about animal testing in them."

"Thank you," said Emily, staring at the front of the leaflet. It was a flyer trying to bring attention to the issue of cosmetics research on animals. A national campaigning group based in Manchester had produced it. Emily's face dropped in dismay when she saw the pictures inside. Staring out at her was a beagle's face pressed up against the bars of a cage.

Bob and Carole Parker were in the office together checking through some paperwork when Neil and Emily got home. "We found it," shouted Neil, as he crashed in through the door. "I've got a number to call."

"There's a picture, too," said Emily. "We're sure it's the same dog. She's called Bella."

"Let's see the picture," said Bob. He looked at it closely.

"See that bit there, Dad," said Emily. "The way the white sweeps round."

Bob nodded. "Yep, it's certainly similar. Well done. Give it a try!"

Neil tried the number. "It's ringing." He waited, holding the phone close to his ear. "No one's answering it."

"Keep trying," urged Emily. "They may be outside."

Neil hung on, growing increasingly impatient with every unanswered ring. He put the phone down and tried the number again. Still no reply. "It's no good," he said. "The owner's definitely not in."

"Never mind," said Carole. "Try again later. Don't be too disappointed. You've already made a fantastic breakthrough."

Neil shrugged, trying not to show how upset he was. "It would explain the dog taking a shine to Emily, wouldn't it? You know, if she'd belonged to a girl her age."

"It's possible," said Bob. "You'll also be interested to learn that Glen's coming over at lunchtime. He's got some news about what the research centre is up to. It seems that they definitely *are* using some animals to test cosmetics."

"I knew it," said Neil, perking up. "We've got to get the puppies out of there." He ran towards the door. "I'm going to see what Kate knows."

"Wait!" called out Carole. "Kate is . . . Oh, never mind."

Neil had already disappeared.

Kate was out walking some of the boarding dogs. After a frustrating half an hour kicking his heels, Neil rushed out of the house when he saw Glen arriving on a bike. Kate arrived back just as Neil was eagerly ushering him into the kitchen.

"Thanks for dropping by, Glen," Bob told him. "I think Neil and Emily have got some questions for you about last night's meeting."

"You've found something out, haven't you?" asked Neil.

"Well," said Glen, nodding, "as Kate may have already told you, we now know for definite that Universal Laboratories has recently agreed a contract with a large international cosmetics company called Carefree Products. They're going to use animals to test a new range of waterproof mascara that the company currently has in development."

Bob interrupted. "I'm sorry, Glen, but does this involve dogs? Neil seems to have the idea that the beagle we found the other day has come from there. He thinks the research centre could be using her puppies."

"I really don't think so, Neil," said Glen. "Although hundreds of animals are still used every year for cosmetics tests in this country, they're mostly guinea pigs and mice and rabbits. Dogs are only used for medical research now."

"Well, couldn't they be using them for that?" Neil persisted.

"And dogs and pets do get stolen for research," added Emily. "It says so in all the leaflets."

Neil reached under the table and stroked Sam's head. There was no way he would let anybody steal his dog.

Glen continued his explanation. "Dogs are

stolen sometimes, but not in this country. All animals used in laboratories have to come from special breeding establishments. I'm really pretty sure your beagle and her puppies wouldn't have been stolen by the research centre. It would be too much of a risk for them to take. There are some very strict laws governing exactly what these research stations can and can't use."

"No one's going to steal my Fudge, are they?" said Sarah.

Glen smiled. "Definitely not, but we are trying to stop lots of rabbits and mice and hamsters like Fudge being unnecessarily hurt and killed."

"What can we do?" asked Carole.

"We want to make sure that everyone knows what's going on. If there's enough adverse publicity, the company and the centre may be persuaded to abandon these kinds of tests. It's early enough for us to create a lot of pressure on them to give up this kind of work. There are lots of other methods of research these people can use." Glen rummaged about in his bag and pulled out a bundle of bulging folders.

Kate leant over Glen's shoulder and opened

up some of the folders. She spread some leaflets across the table. "There are a lot of things we can all do to help. There's going to be a large protest rally outside the centre on Saturday. We need help collecting signatures for a petition."

"Most of all we need people to start boycotting all Carefree products," said Glen.

Neil and Emily picked up some of the leaflets. "Hey!" said Emily. "We've got some of this stuff in the bathroom!"

"There are a lot of companies who don't test their make-up on animals at all," said Kate. "We should all be using those. I've got a list here."

"I'll make a copy of that," said Carole. "I'm sure your aunt uses some of these items, Emily."

Emily turned to Glen. Neil could see that his sister's brain was already working overtime. "We could make some huge placards for the rally. And I bet we can collect loads of signatures too."

"I can help, too," said Sarah. "I'll do a giant picture of Fudge."

"Great," said Glen. "Kate will keep you in touch with any new plans or developments. Do you think you and Carole will be able to get to the rally, Bob?"

"We'll certainly try. One of us will have to stay at the kennels, but we'll do all we can."

"This is so exciting," cried Emily. "We can really make a difference!"

"We can – but not right now," said Bob, getting up from the table. "I think we'd better get back to work . . ."

Sarah turned to Kate. "I want Glen to see Baa. Will he come?"

Glen grinned. "Sure, I'll come. Kate's told me all about him."

"I'm going to start my placard now," said Emily. "I need to come up with a brilliant slogan. Have you got any ideas, Neil?"

But Neil wasn't really listening. He was still thinking about Bella and her puppies. He wasn't completely reassured by what Glen had said. "You know, Glen, there *are* dogs there," he blurted out. "We heard them barking, didn't we, Em? Is there any way we can find out for sure that they're not using beagles?"

"You don't give up, do you?" said Glen, smiling. "The barking you heard might have been guard dogs. They've got a couple of very fierce Dobermans patrolling day and night. If you're still really worried, I'll see what I can find out. That man who crashed into my mum the other day was actually the centre's publicity officer. They're usually very careful about the information they release, but I might be able to find out something. I'll give you a call about it."

Neil watched from the doorstep as Sarah dragged Glen and Kate away to visit Baa. Kate called to him. "Are you coming, Neil? We're giving him a run in the exercise field."

Neil shook his head. He wasn't in the mood. "No, I'm going to help Emily." He felt Sam brush against his legs. His alert, eager eyes were looking up expectantly at him. "Did you hear the word *run*, boy? Off you go then. Go and join them." He watched Sam race after Sarah and Kate.

Emily was already waving big bits of paper about in the kitchen. "Come on, Neil. I've got some great ideas for posters."

"In a minute," Neil replied. "I'm just going to phone Mrs Thompson again."

Chapter Seven

"**H**ave you tried getting hold of Bella's owners yet this morning, Neil?" asked Carole at breakfast.

Neil nodded. "Yes. I tried three times last night, and again this morning. There's still no reply. I'll try again in a minute."

"Finish your breakfast first or you'll be hungry later," Carole told him. Neil reluctantly went back to eating his nut clusters.

"Hello? Can everyone please hurry up?" Emily was hovering in the doorway with a large scroll of card tucked under her arm and a handful of thick marker pens. "I need this table to finish my placard."

Bob Parker put his head round the kitchen

door. "There's a visitor here for you, Neil."

Neil jumped up as his father showed a small blonde-haired woman into the kitchen. "This is Mrs Paget, Glen's mum," Bob said, introducing her.

Mrs Paget stretched out her hand. "Call me Wendy, please."

"And I'm Carole. Please, sit down. You've already met Neil and Emily," she said. "That's Sarah down there, I think," said Carole, pointing under the table. Sarah's foot and Sam's feathery black tail could just be seen poking out into view.

Mrs Paget smiled. "Sorry to barge in so early. Glen was going to phone Neil – but as I was passing . . ."

"Did he find something out?" Neil interrupted eagerly. "He was going to call the man from the research centre."

Mrs Paget sat down at the table. "Yes, the man with the important meeting to go to. I phoned him last night myself. I needed to check something with him about the accident any-way. He had a police incident number I needed for my insurance claim."

"Was he still Mr Angry?" asked Neil.

Wendy smiled. "Well, he wasn't very

forthcoming to start with, but it helped that we'd met and he knew who I was. He wasn't prepared to go into details with me about any medical research they might or might not be doing involving animals. But when I mentioned beagle puppies, he did tell me something very interesting. It seems that a few days ago a man phoned up, actually trying to sell some beagle puppies to them!"

"I knew it! They've got them!" said Neil, energetically.

"Wait, hold on," said Mrs Paget. "The centre refused the man point blank, of course. In fact, Mr Pritchard wondered if the man was genuine at all, since all the animals they do use for experiments have to be legally obtained from specially licensed breeding establishments. He suspected the man might be some activist trying to discredit the centre. I assured him that the man wasn't anything to do with the protests."

"No," said Emily, grimly. "The man's genuine – whoever he is. And he still has Bella's puppies! We've got to find him."

Bob Parker nodded. "This does look like the lead you've both been waiting for. They could well be the beagle's pups. It's too much of a coincidence and no reputable breeder would try and sell a litter in that fashion."

"I was reading through that leaflet Emily brought from the library," said Carole. "It can cost a lot to buy a beagle from a proper breeder. He must have been hoping to make a lot of money out of those puppies."

"What do you think he'll do now?" asked Emily. "They won't be worth much without pedigree documents."

"I doubt he'll just dump them," said Bob. "Even without documents they're worth something to him. He might try to sell them as pets – especially if he's gone to the trouble and risk of stealing them. It's looking increasingly likely that Bella was stolen. She could have escaped from wherever the puppies are still being kept."

"But how are we going to find them?" asked Neil desperately.

"He might advertise them," suggested Mrs Paget. "There are lots of ads in the papers. And the post office in Padsham is full of For Sale notices advertising pets."

"Good idea," said Bob.

"We could try pet shops, too," exclaimed Emily.

"It looks like you and Neil have got your work cut out, Emily," said Carole. Then she turned to Mrs Paget. "Thanks so much for all your help."

"Yes, you've been great," said Neil. He glanced at the kitchen clock on the wall. "I'll try that number again in Middlesbrough before we start looking. It's been at least half an hour since I last called."

A few minutes later an elated Neil charged back into the room. "I got through! I got through! Someone answered."

"You spoke to Bella's owner? What did she say?" Emily asked excitedly.

"It wasn't Mrs Thompson. It was a neighbour. She was feeding the cats when she heard the phone. Mrs Thompson and her daughter are on holiday. And no, they haven't found Bella, she's still missing. They're coming back on Sunday. I've left a message for her with our number."

"That's great, Neil," said Carole.

Wendy Paget got up. "Thanks for the coffee, anyway. I'm glad things are working out. Could I just take a quick look at Bella before I go? I'd like to see her again."

"Of course," said Bob Parker. "She's doing fine. You'll see a big difference in her."

"We'll take you," said Neil.

"I'm coming too," said Sarah.

Neil opened the main door of the rescue centre and beckoned Wendy Paget inside.

"Bella may be sleeping," said Emily, following behind them.

"Baa won't be," said Sarah, giggling. "He's too bouncy!"

In fact, neither of the dogs was asleep. The beagle was out of her basket and was sniffing the cocker spaniel puppy through the wire mesh that separated their pens. Little Baa's tail was wagging furiously and she whimpered with delight.

"I think Bella has really taken to Baa," said Neil. "Emily's idea to put them in pens next to each other was brilliant. Having a friend has really helped Bella's recovery."

Wendy knelt down. "Yes, she certainly looks a lot happier and more relaxed. I bet King Street is like a hotel to her considering what she's been through."

"Dad reckons we can take her out into the exercise field for the first time this afternoon," said Emily. "She's got a lot of her energy back now." Emily poked her fingers through the wire mesh and the beagle came towards her. She gently touched the dog's white chest and ruffled her coat. Bella was getting stronger every day.

Shortly after lunch, Neil and Emily were on their bikes and heading into Compton. "I think we should check the pet shops first," said Neil. "I don't think they'll have anything in a big High Street shop, but there's a shabby-looking one near the library. They were selling kittens in there the other day."

"OK," Emily agreed. "Then we'll check the newsagents and corner shops. I've brought a petition with me to see if we can get some signatures for the Carefree Products boycott campaign too."

But the visits to the pet shops revealed nothing. No one had tried to sell a litter of young beagle puppies to either of them.

"You'd be best trying the local papers," Mr Kemp in the High Street pet shop had told them. "The new *Advertiser* comes out at lunchtime." He'd also wanted to know all about the research centre. "If you leave me copies of the petition here, I'm sure a lot of my customers will sign – they're all animal lovers. I had no idea what was going on there. I thought the place was developing giant tomatoes, that sort of thing – not testing cosmetics."

As the day wore on, Neil became hotter and more discouraged. "We've visited every newsagent in Compton now, except for Mrs Smedley, but she's on the way home. We could have bought everything from caravans to cockatoos – but no puppies," he groaned.

"Two Cokes please, Mrs Smedley," said Emily, as they flopped across the counter of their local newsagent. "And have you got the *Advertiser* yet? You keep copies here, don't you?"

Mrs Smedley was filling a jar with sticky sweets from a large carton. She nodded and wiped her palms on her overall. "It's just come in. You two look exhausted. What have you been up to?"

Neil explained about the beagle puppies.

"I haven't got any adverts for puppies at all," the woman said. "But I'll give you a ring if anything turns up. And you can leave me some of those petitions too. I'm sure a lot of people coming in will want to sign." Mrs Smedley had always been a good friend to King Street Kennels.

"Thanks for the paper, Mrs Smedley," said Neil, as they left. "We'll keep you posted with any developments."

Back at King Street Kennels, Neil and Emily found a huge plate of sandwiches on the kitchen table. There was also a note from their mother reminding them that it was Kate's birthday.

"We'd better go and give Kate her card," said Emily.

They found Kate busy cleaning out one of the pens in Kennel Block Two. Emily handed her the coloured envelope and shouted, "Happy birthday!"

"Thanks, guys," she said, reading the card. "That's really thoughtful of you."

Neil slapped Kate's back, playfully. "You should be taking it easy today. I can't believe you've actually turned up for work on your birthday! That's dedication to dogs for you."

Kate blushed. "I can't help it! And I'm going out with Glen later, so I've got something to look forward to."

Neil nudged Emily in the ribs.

Kate blushed again and said something hurriedly to change the subject. "I've just looked in on Bella. She's really perking up. Sarah says you're going to take her out later."

"As soon as we've looked at this newspaper," said Neil, waving the *Advertiser* at her. "We're trying to track down the puppies. We picked up the new issue in Compton – we couldn't wait for it to arrive out here in the sticks! See you later. And happy birthday!"

"Good luck," said Kate. "Hope you come up with something."

Neil and Emily spread the newspaper out on the kitchen table and eagerly scanned the For Sale columns.

Neil's face burst into a smile. "Listen to this!" he said. *"Beautiful beagle pups for sale. Good family pets."*

"That's it! We might have found them, Neil," said Emily, excitedly.

"You try the number, Em."

Neil listened as Emily dialled the number. Then she nodded encouragingly to him. Someone must have answered. "Hello. I understand you have some beagle puppies for sale. Can you tell me how old they are, please?" Her face fell as she listened. "Oh, I see, um, yes. Well no, thank you." She put the receiver down.

"What is it?" asked Neil anxiously.

Emily shook her head. "They were too young. Only two weeks old. They couldn't be the right ones."

Neil was crestfallen. "Another dead end. I can't stand much more of this!"

"At least we've found Bella's owners," said Emily.

"I suppose so." Neil looked uncertain. "It looks as if we're never going to find her puppies, though. I'm really worried – that man may just dump them if he can't find a buyer. Even if we do trace him, we might be too late."

Chapter Eight

Wednesday was another hot sultry day at King Street. The dogs were feeling the heat and an unusually quiet hush had descended over the kennels. The dogs lay stretched out in their pens and greeted Kate and Neil with quiet, grateful wags instead of the usual round of barking as they were brought fresh water.

"How's the campaign going?" Neil asked her.

"Glen says that about thirty students are going to the rally and that they've also managed to get a lot of support from local people. There should be a good turnout on Saturday. The press will be there too," she told Neil. "By the

81

way, where's Sarah?" she asked as they walked over to the rescue centre. "She's usually here to see Baa at this time."

"She's sort of helping Emily with a placard, I think," said Neil. "But her colouring-in isn't too hot."

Just then Sarah came running up. "Kate, Kate! Wait for me. Am I too late?"

Kate smiled. "No, here you are." She handed Sarah a bowl. "This is Baa's. Neil, can you take Bella's food for me? I'll fetch the water."

Sarah turned excitedly to Neil. "Baa can sit now, when I tell him. He does for his bowl anyway. Kate showed me how."

"We'll give Bella hers first," said Neil.

The beagle was already sitting patiently waiting when Neil opened her pen. Her short coat gleamed and looked healthy again thanks to Kate's grooming, and her large brown eyes were bright and alert. She watched Neil put down her bowl. She waited for his command before moving. "Eat up, girl!" Neil told her. With a happy tail-wag she moved eagerly to the bowl and began to eat.

Then Neil opened Baa's pen. The cocker spaniel was charging round and round excitedly. He began to dash backwards and forwards towards Sarah. "Baa, sit!" said Sarah sternly, holding up his bowl. "Baa, sit!"

Baa sat as still as he could, trembling with excitement.

Neil was impressed. "You've done really well, Squirt," he told her, taking her hand. "Come on, let's go and help Emily."

Neil spent a frustrating day on Thursday worrying about Bella. He also helped Emily add to a pile of placards in preparation for the rally. On Friday afternoon, Neil was in the rescue centre after a morning spent collecting signatures for the Carefree Products boycott petition in Compton. He was watching Bella playing with Baa in her pen when Bob Parker came over with Sarah to join him. Baa wriggled away from Bella and charged back towards his own pen. Sarah picked him up and cuddled him.

Bob handed Neil the latest edition of the *Compton News*. "I thought you might like to see this. I know you've been waiting for it."

"Great!" Neil took the paper, quickly found the For Sale section and scanned down the column. Moments later he closed the pages and handed it back. "Nothing."

Bob put a hand on Neil's shoulder. "I'm sorry, Neil. But it was a long shot, wasn't it? You might have to accept that you may never find Bella's puppies."

Neil nodded but didn't reply.

"You and Emily have already done brilliantly finding Bella and making sure she's safe. Mrs Thompson's going to be over the moon to get her dog back after all this time."

"I know." Neil watched Sarah playing with Baa and smiled.

Bob Parker nodded in Sarah's direction. "She's getting very fond of him, isn't she?" he whispered. Sarah was so involved in playing with Baa that she was not listening to the conversation going on above her head.

"We can't keep him, can we Dad?" said Neil.

"No. I just hope Sarah realizes that. I think I'd better have a word with her."

Neil watched as his father helped Sarah put Baa back into his pen.

Bob took hold of Sarah's hand. "Darling," he said, quietly. "Try not to get too attached to Baa, will you? He'll probably have to leave us soon."

"What do you mean?" Sarah's bottom lip began to tremble.

"Baa will probably be going to new owners. I'm afraid we can't keep him here for ever."

Sarah looked down at the spaniel puppy scrambling up at the wire mesh and trying to touch her. "But I love him," she said.

Neil swallowed hard. He knew how she must be feeling. Although he was older now, part of him still wanted to keep every dog that came into the rescue centre too.

Bob gave Sarah a hug. "I know you love him, darling. But we already have Sam. And Fudge."

Sarah started crying and ran past them both. Bob shrugged at Neil, then followed her out of the rescue centre to try to calm her down.

Neil sighed. Sarah was too young to understand that they couldn't give every puppy a home themselves. Just then, he felt a wet nose pushed against his hand. It was Sam. "Hello, boy." Neil stroked the collie's soft ears. "How do you always seem to know when I'm feeling low?" He bent down and hugged his dog. "You know what, a walk would probably do me good. Come on, let's go."

As he turned to leave, Neil almost bumped into Emily.

"Neil!" she said. "I've been looking everywhere for you."

"What is it?" asked Neil.

"It's Mrs Smedley," she said excitedly. "She's just phoned. A man came into the shop and left an advert to be put up in the window. He's got some beagle puppies for sale! She's given me the number on the card. It's a Padsham number."

A few minutes later, they were back in the house. Neil picked up the phone. Slowly he pressed the numbers. Emily gripped the table anxiously next to him. "Is anyone there?" she whispered.

Neil shook his head. Then he nodded. Someone had answered. "Hello. Have you got some beagle puppies for sale?" he asked, trying to keep his voice calm. "Could I come and see them, please? What, now? Before six. Right. OK, we're coming. Where? Yes, I think I know. Goodbye."

Neil put the phone down. He was shaking. He turned to Emily. "I think he has Bella's puppies! They're about eight weeks old. We've got to go and see them now because he's going out soon. He lives off the main Padsham to Compton road, past the Beedham turning. Come on, we've got to hurry."

Just as they grabbed their bikes, Carole Parker turned into the kennels in the Range Rover. She wound down the window. "Just a minute. Where are you going? Don't be late for dinner."

"We won't. See you, Mum," said Neil, pedalling away.

"We won't be long," shouted Emily, waving.

Emily looked at Neil as they waited to turn into the main road. "Where is this place? How far is it?"

"Follow me," said Neil. He knew the turning. They must have ridden past it hundreds of times on their way to Padsham, but neither of them had ever been down it.

After a quarter of an hour's hard pedalling they left the main road and turned into a narrow, winding lane. The smallholding the man had described was called Four Acres and was supposed to be just a few minutes down the lane.

The main road had been busy with early evening traffic. The sudden quietness and remoteness of the lane was a little unnerving but Neil kept going. "It's not far now," he called back to Emily.

They passed a small clump of trees and then, as they turned the next bend, they saw it. A rusty metal sign hung from a post at the roadside. The property was bordered by a rotting picket fence, the gate was propped open, and a weed-covered drive led to some buildings beyond. The smallholding seemed to consist of a bungalow and a few dilapidated outbuildings. The yard was strewn with pieces of broken tractor.

Neil turned to Emily. "I don't like the look of this place."

Emily shook her head. "We can't go back now."

They left their bikes by the road and walked towards the bungalow. A rusty red van, its bonnet open, was standing in the driveway. Neil looked at his watch. It was ten to six. They'd only just made it in time.

Emily knocked on the door. A man opened it. He looked younger than he'd sounded on the phone. He was wearing overalls, and his long, dark hair hung round his unshaven face. He was wiping his hands on a dirty rag.

"We've come about the puppies, Mr . . ." said Neil. The man didn't give him a name so Neil continued, hesitantly. "I phoned earlier. We got here as quickly as we could."

"Come in," the man said, glancing towards the van. "I've been doing some work on her. I was just about to clean myself up."

Neil and Emily followed him into the small kitchen, trying not to show their unease.

"You've only just caught me. I'm on my way out, so you'll have to be quick. Wait here, I'll fetch him for you."

"Er, would it be possible to see all the litter, please? How many are there?" Neil asked.

The man shook his head. "Three. But sorry, son, they're all spoken for except one. Not much point seeing the other two."

Emily stepped forward. "What about the mother? Could we see her, please?"

The man looked at Emily. "Know a lot about dogs, do we?"

"Oh, no," said Neil quickly. "Not really. Our mum does. We're looking for a surprise present for her."

"Well, you're out of luck with the puppies' mother, I'm afraid. My friend has . . . just taken her out for a long walk. They need a good bit of exercise, don't they?"

"Oh yes," said Emily. "And grooming and everything."

"Well, do you want to see this puppy or not?"

"Yes, please," said Neil and Emily, nodding.

The man left the kitchen. Neil watched him through the window walking towards the outbuildings. The man paused and glanced back. Neil quickly moved out of sight. "He doesn't want us to see where they're kept," whispered Neil.

Emily nodded. "That was rubbish about the long walk. And why didn't he give us his name?"

The man returned in a few minutes with a very young beagle puppy clutched in his hands. He cleared a place on the table and put it down. "There you go. He's a fine little fellow – good stock and temperament. He'll make a nice pet. Go on, pick him up," he said to Emily.

The puppy was very thin with a bulging stomach. He cowered, shivering on the table, scratching and slipping on the smooth surface with its tiny claws. Emily gently scooped him up and held him against her. Softly she stroked the white markings on his forehead with her finger as the trembling puppy nuzzled closer. "You're a sweet little thing, aren't you?" she whispered.

"He's a bit shy in here," said the man. "You should see him with the others though. Always raring to go, that one. Well, what do you think? Do you want him?"

Neil nodded and smiled, trying not to show his concern for the puppy. "He's lovely but we haven't got any money with us. Can we come back tomorrow?"

"That'll be fine," said the man. "I want cash, mind. Fifty quid. Come round about this time."

Neil held out his hand. "Thank you. I'm sure he'll have a good home with us."

Reluctantly Emily handed the puppy back to the man as he hurried them out of the door. "I'm running late. See you tomorrow."

Neil and Emily walked silently back down the drive. "Poor little thing," Emily whispered when they reached the bikes. "Did you see its stomach?"

Neil nodded. He was seething inside. "It hadn't been wormed. It's obviously not being looked after properly, poor thing. I bet they're being kept in awful conditions."

"I don't think he knows anything at all about dogs," said Emily.

"We've got to see the others, Emily. They may be in an even worse state."

Emily nodded.

"I think we should wait until he's driven past. Then we can come back and find those puppies."

Neil and Emily raced to the small clump of trees they'd passed earlier. They dragged their bikes off the road and crouched down. Overhead the crows were returning to roost. Their harsh cries broke the silence of the balmy evening. "We're going to be so late home," Emily whispered.

"This is more important," said Neil. "Listen, he's coming."

The red van tore past them with a trail of fumes. When it had disappeared from sight, Neil and Emily dragged their bikes back up to the road and rushed back to the smallholding. It didn't take them long to find the puppies. As Neil peered through the broken panes of one of the small sheds, a chorus of little yaps and cries broke out.

"Quick, Emily, over here!" he cried.

As he peered into the gloom he could make out three puppies. They were tumbling over each other to get to the door, but at least they weren't lying sick and cowering in a corner. He could see a dish of water but the whole place looked as though it hadn't been cleaned out for some time. There were empty cardboard boxes on the floor but no proper bedding.

"We've got to get them out of there," said Emily.

Neil shook his head. "We can't – we'll never get this padlock open. And we don't know for certain that they're Bella's. There's no way of proving it."

"Bella could prove it," said Emily. "The pups would come to her. They won't have forgotten her."

"You're right. That's brilliant. We'll take her tomorrow before anyone's up and see how they react. I'm sure she's up to a decent walk now. Come on, let's get out of here."

Chapter Nine

The rest of the Parker family was sitting in the kitchen eating supper when Neil and Emily got home. "Sorry we're late, Mum," said Neil as he sidled into his place at the table. "We've had a great afternoon."

"We got loads of signatures for the petition," Emily added, without being too specific about where they'd actually got them from.

In fact Carole and Bob Parker weren't about to start asking questions. They were too anxious about Sarah, who was sitting staring at her plate, refusing to eat anything.

"Come on, darling," said Carole. "You've got to eat. You've always known that we couldn't keep Baa. We've already got Sam and Fudge."

"We haven't even found a home for him yet," said Bob. "He's going to be with us a bit longer, I'm sure. But you wouldn't want him to always be at the rescue centre, would you? He needs a proper home and he won't always be a puppy. Before long he'll be grown up like Sam."

"Perhaps you could spend a bit more time with Neil and Sam," said Carole, looking at Neil. "Sam needs a lot of love from all of us, not just from Neil."

"Sure," said Neil, joining in. "And you can come to the woods and I'll show you all his favourite places. Hey look," he added, grinning. "Sam *wants* you to spend time with him." Sam had sat up when he heard his name, and was now nuzzling up against Sarah.

"Can we go now?" asked Sarah, perking up.

"You'll have to hurry up and eat something first. It'll soon be your bedtime," said Carole, smiling her thanks at Neil.

That night Neil found it hard to get to sleep. His mind was racing as he thought about the next morning. The rally against the research centre suddenly seemed less important now they'd found the beagle pups. Neil woke before the alarm went off and silently crept into Emily's room. She was already awake and dressed. They slipped outside, leaving the door on the latch. Their biggest problem would be getting Bella out of her pen without disturbing the other dogs in the rescue centre.

Emily slowly eased the rescue centre door open just enough for Neil to squeeze through. Neil tiptoed inside, trying not to make too much noise as he made his way along the aisle towards Bella's pen. Although some of the dogs stirred to greet him, they didn't bark. Some of them looked up, yawned and curled back up in their baskets. Baa scampered up to the fence when he saw him. Neil held his breath. An enthusiastic greeting from Baa might ruin everything. He scratched the puppy's chin through the mesh and willed him to go back to his basket. After what seemed like an eternity, the little dog sleepily padded back to his basket and curled up. Neil let out a huge sigh of relief.

Neil stepped inside Bella's pen. She was sleeping so soundly that she didn't wake up straight away. "Come on, girl," he whispered to Bella as he clipped on her lead. "We're going to find your puppies."

A minute later, Neil emerged from the rescue centre clutching Bella's lead.

"What took you so long?" hissed Emily.

"Puppy problems," said Neil.

They crossed the exercise field and slipped out into the fields beyond. The ground was wet with early dew and a white floating mist stretched as far as they could see.

"You are sure about this path, aren't you?" asked Emily, suspiciously.

Neil nodded. "We just keep on to the woods and then follow the path which runs along that small stream. And then it's straight across fields again. I've brought the map anyway." They'd found a footpath on the map, which led across country from the woods near King Street Kennels to the lane where the smallholding was. It cut off quite a bit of the journey and would be better for Bella than trudging down the main road.

"Bella's enjoying it," said Emily. The beagle looked up and wagged her tail when she heard her name. She'd kept her nose to the ground all the way. She behaved well on the lead, keeping to heel and not straining, but Neil sensed that she longed to be running free.

At last they reached the road. "We turn right now," said Neil, looking at the map. "Just a little way along and Four Acres should be on our left."

"I hope that man isn't up yet," said Emily.

"We'll have to hope he's having a lie-in," said Neil.

They walked quickly along the road. Suddenly, as they rounded a bend, the familiar run-down buildings appeared in front of them. They stopped for a moment to catch their breath. Neil knelt down and ruffled Bella's ears. "Are you ready for this, girl?" She looked up at him eagerly.

Emily smiled. "She's all right."

As they drew nearer to the drive, Bella seemed to hesitate. Then she began to sniff the ground in a more urgent way.

"What is it, Bella?" whispered Neil.

"I think she recognizes the place," said Emily. "Shall we let her off the lead?"

"I suppose so. We need to see what she does."

"I don't think she'll go far," said Neil, slipping off her lead.

The beagle seemed to hang back for a moment. Then as they turned into the gateway, she suddenly darted forward with her nose to the ground.

"Here, girl!" called Neil in dismay as the beagle sped away from them, down the drive.

"Oh, no!" Emily whispered.

"Look at that!" cried Neil. "Straight there! She's going to those outbuildings. There's *no way* this is the first time she's been to this place."

"We've got to get her back," said Emily. "Before she wakes the puppies."

As they ran along the drive, Neil kept glancing upwards, hoping that the man didn't appear in the window of the house. Bella reached the shed door. She was scratching and whining. The puppies were awake now. Their tiny yelps seemed terribly loud in the still morning.

"Bella. Here!" called Neil. As he ran forward with her lead, the door of the bungalow opened.

The man stood there in his vest, blearily rubbing his eyes. "What the . . .?" he began. He caught sight of Neil and Bella.

"Quickly!" screamed Emily.

Neil put the lead on Bella and dragged her away. He began to run and he didn't look back. Emily was running too.

"Hey! You . . ." They heard the man's voice bellowing after them. "What are you up to? Come back here!"

Neil and Emily kept running, down the road towards the footpath, praying that the man wouldn't follow. As they stumbled across the fields, Neil thought thankfully it was a good thing they'd taken this route. On the road they'd have stood no chance – the man would easily have caught up with them in his car.

They didn't stop until they reached the woods. Emily glanced back. "It's all right. He's not coming. He hasn't followed us."

They stood still for a minute, trying to get their breath back. "He'll have seen Bella and recognized us," said Neil. "He'll know we're on to him."

"We'll have to tell Mum and Dad," said Emily.

Neil nodded. "You know what this means –

he'll get rid of them now for sure, as quickly as he can. The puppies are the only thing linking him to Bella – he can't risk that. He'd be in trouble for stealing a dog. He'll have to dump them straight away. Anywhere. Possibly even the river . . . We've got to stop him!"

be'll get rid of them now for sure as quickly as he can. The quickest way to be out of trouble for owning a dog. He'll have to dump them anywhere, anywhere. Possibly even the river if we've got to stop

Chapter Ten

It was nearly nine o'clock by the time Neil and Emily got home. They'd already been missed, but there was no time for recriminations. Once Bob and Carole had heard what Neil and Emily had to say about the beagle pups, they sprang into action. Carole phoned the police while Bob put Bella safely back in the rescue centre. He told Neil and Emily to wait in the car for him.

Minutes later, Bob Parker was beside them. "The police are going to get there as quickly as they can," he said. "But most of their men are busy at the rally."

"We've got to get over there, Dad," urged Neil. "We need to watch the place in case the man gets rid of the puppies before they arrive. He'll want to destroy the evidence."

Bob jumped into the car and reversed out of the drive onto the road.

"Take the left for Padsham," shouted Emily from the back seat. "And then it's another left turn before Beedham. We'll show you. Watch out for the tight corners, though!"

Bob gripped the steering wheel, staring ahead. "Can you see the place from the road?" he asked, as they sped along the narrow country lanes.

"Yes," said Neil. "But he'll be able to see us too."

"OK, I'll drive right past. You two look out and see if there's any sign of him."

"I'll check if his van's there," said Neil.

Bob slowed down as they passed the run-down smallholding. Neil and Emily strained out of the window.

"He's there!" screamed Emily. "And he's carrying a large box to the van. It must be the puppies!"

"We're too late, Dad!" Neil shouted. "You've got to turn round."

Bob quickly pulled over to the side of the road. "The lane's too narrow for us to turn round. Keep watching him. We don't know which way he's going to go yet."

"He's put the box in the van and now he's getting in," said Neil, urgently. "That box looked very small. The puppies will be crushed."

"Do something!" pleaded Emily.

Bob threw the Range Rover into reverse. "I'll try and block him," he shouted.

It was too late. The red van shot out of the drive and sped towards the main road.

"He must know we're after him. Don't worry, we won't let him get away. Hold on!" Bob told them as he reversed into the drive and moved off after the van.

For a time, they lost sight of the van completely as they raced down the twisting road. "He's vanished!" said Neil, desperately.

"It's just these bends," said Bob. "He can't be far ahead. We'll see him on the straight. Here, catch this." He tossed the mobile phone to Neil. "Get onto Sergeant Moorhead. Tell him what's happening."

"We don't know which way he's gone," cried Emily, as they reached the main road.

Bob craned forward over the wheel. "There," he shouted, catching sight of a speck of red up ahead. "He's heading for Padsham town centre."

Neil watched the road as Emily made a frantic call to the police on the mobile. He was thinking about the puppies being tossed about in the cardboard box in the back of the van. "I'll kill him," he muttered. "If those puppies are hurt, I'll . . ."

A moment later a police car, its siren wailing, tore past them on the other side of the road.

"Oh no!" cried Neil. "They're going the wrong way!"

"Look," shouted Emily suddenly, pointing at the van – which seemed to be getting closer. "We're gaining on him. He's slowing down!"

"There's something happening up ahead," said Bob.

"There are people there in the road. Look!" Neil shouted. "It's the rally! Excellent!"

"They've blocked the main road," said Bob.

Ahead of the Range Rover, the red van had screeched to a stop. Several people with placards taking part in the rally had spilled out from the research centre driveway onto the main road. The crowd was a lot bigger than either Neil or Emily had expected. There were several policemen at the periphery of the crowd trying to move them off the road. A television news camera crew was recording the chanting of slogans near the main gate.

The Range Rover pulled up a couple of metres behind the van. Bob smiled. "We've got him now!"

"Watch it, Dad!" Neil warned. "He's trying to turn round. He's going to come back on the other side."

The red van backed onto the grass verge, crashing into the *Universal Laboratories* sign. The van began to spin its wheels, revving its engine ready to surge away.

Bob saw his chance. "Hold on," he shouted to Neil and Emily. He quickly swung the Range Rover in front of the van, blocking its escape.

For a second the man in the red van seemed to hesitate, unsure what to do next. They were so close they could see his grim face scowling at them.

Suddenly, the crowd seemed to surge forward towards them.

"Look," said Emily. "There's Kate and Glen."

Neil felt his heart racing, but there was no time to be scared. He leapt from the car and shouted across to Glen. "It's him! The man who stole the puppies! Stop him!"

The man had jumped down from the van. For

a second he swayed like a frightened rabbit, wondering which way to bolt, and then headed towards the open fields. Glen broke from the crowd and raced after him, followed by a policeman and Kate.

Bob Parker clambered out of the Range Rover over the passenger seat – his own door was blocked by the van. "Stay here!" he shouted to Neil and Emily, as he joined in the chase. "Get the puppies."

Neil and Emily watched as Glen threw himself at the fleeing man and brought him roughly down to the ground.

They ran together to the back of the red van but the doors wouldn't open. They were jammed solid against the broken signpost. Neil pulled at the broken post and sign. "They're trapped!"

People from the crowd came forward.

"We've got to get the puppies out of there!" Emily shouted. "They might be hurt! They'll suffocate in this heat."

Suddenly Neil felt an arm on his shoulder. "Let me help."

Neil turned. It was Mr Pritchard, the man from Universal Laboratories. As Mr Pritchard and a few students from the crowd struggled to free the van's doors, the camera crew closed in on them to record the incident.

Finally, Neil wrenched open the back doors. A sealed cardboard box lay on its side where it had fallen over during the bumpy journey. Neil and Emily could hear scratching and whimpering.

Emily began to pull away the heavy parcel tape that sealed the box lid. "They must be terrified!" she cried.

"They'd better not be hurt," muttered Neil.

Emily's fingers were trembling. From inside the box the yelping and scratching grew louder. At last, she tore open the lid. Three small beagle pups leapt up at the sides, scrabbling to get out.

"Are they all right?" asked Emily, anxiously.

"I think so," whispered Neil. He put his hand into the box. Little wet noses and tongues snuffled and grabbed at his fingers. He could hardly believe it. They'd done it. They'd rescued the puppies! It was all over. Gently, he lifted out one of the struggling, yapping bundles and passed it to Emily.

"Oh, you're beautiful," gasped Emily, as she held the soft, short-haired beagle puppy on her knee. The little pup licked her hand and buried its white muzzle into her T-shirt.

The crowd broke into applause.

Kate appeared at Neil's side and patted him on the back. "Wow!" she said, laughing. "What an entrance! I thought you weren't going to make it to the rally when I didn't see you earlier on."

Neil mopped his brow. "We were . . . held up!" He lifted another brown and white bundle on to his knee. Big brown eyes stared up at him. A long thin tail wagged. "You're OK, little feller," he said, as the puppy began to chew his finger. "You're safe now."

That afternoon, three washed and gleaming puppies were reunited with Bella in her pen at King Street Kennels. It was a very special moment and Neil and Emily felt quite choked as they watched Bella greet the tumbling playful pups. She sniffed and washed each one in turn, glancing up from time to time.

Carole, Sarah, Bob and Mike Turner all looked on, anxiously.

"She looks so pleased," whispered Emily.

Bella then retreated to her basket and sat watching as the puppies tumbled and jostled round her.

"She seems very proud of them," said Neil.

"Whoops!" laughed Sarah, as one of the puppies rolled against its mother, only to find itself held down by a firm paw and given another good washing.

"Are they going to be all right, Mike?" asked Emily.

"They've been kept in pretty poor conditions. One has an ear infection, another a sore eye. I'll leave some drops and ointment. They all need worming straight away, but once they're cleaned up and are given the right food, they should be fine."

"We're hoping to hear from the owners tomorrow," said Bob.

"Yes, they'll need to get their own vet to look at them again in a few days' time."

After a few more minutes, Bella's puppies grew tired and one by one they flopped down beside their mother. Soon they were all breathing in unison – their eyes tightly closed and their little brown and white bodies heaving gently. With a final contented lick and sniff, Bella sighed and closed her eyes too.

Neil smiled and turned to Emily. "We did it, Em, didn't we? We did it!"

"What's happened to the man who stole Bella?" asked Mike, as he packed his bag.

"Sergeant Moorhead called just before you arrived," said Bob. "The man confessed."

"Of course he did!" said Neil, angrily.

"He was a salesman dealing in second-hand agricultural machine parts who often travelled all over the country. It seems it wasn't the first time he'd done this sort of thing. He'd been involved with a dog-stealing racket in the past, taking animals to order, and he already had one conviction."

"That's awful," gasped Emily.

"He saw another chance for some easy cash when he noticed the pregnant beagle in a park during a trip to Middlesbrough. He couldn't resist it. He thought that beagles were used in research, knew about Universal Laboratories, so he grabbed her. Unfortunately for him, Bella escaped from his farm. He thought he might get found out so he was driven into looking for a quick, cheap sale."

"What will happen to him?" Emily asked.

Bob shrugged. "I'm not sure, but it looks as if the RSPCA will be involved as well. He could be prosecuted for cruelty, as well as theft, considering what he did to Bella and the state he kept the puppies in. Hopefully he'll be banned from ever keeping animals."

That evening, Glen and Kate arrived with news of the rally, and Wendy Paget came with them.

The protest had generated a lot of local support and media attention.

"There should be plenty of pictures in the papers tomorrow," said Kate. "The TV report has already gone out. There were some great shots of Glen holding up a placard and shouting!"

"He was better at catching the beagle thief," said Neil. "Did you see how quickly he caught and tackled him?"

Glen reddened and laughed. "I've just got long legs, that's all!"

Kate hugged him. "You were great!"

"It looks as though the rally did a lot of good all round," said Glen. "Word is coming through that Carefree Products *are* going to cancel their contract with Universal Laboratories. They're going to go abandon this type of testing on animals. All the bad publicity is affecting their reputation."

"That's great news," said Bob.

"I don't think it's going to be long before the government bans cosmetics testing on animals altogether," said Glen.

"You've done brilliantly, too," Kate said to Neil and Emily.

"Yes, Bella looks so contented. Her puppies are lovely," added Glen.

"They're really sweet," said Sarah. "Nearly as nice as Baa."

Wendy Paget suddenly looked at Bob and smiled.

"We've got some news for you, sweetheart," said Bob. He paused. "We've found a home for Baa."

As Sarah's face began to crumple, he took her on to his knee. "No, listen, it couldn't be better. Wendy's going to look after him. Baa is going to live with Wendy and Glen. They've been wanting a puppy for ages."

Wendy knelt down next to them. "I want you to promise to come to tea with us every week," she said. "You'll always be Baa's special friend. We'll be bringing him to your dad's classes when he's old enough, so you'll see him then as well."

Sarah was quiet for a minute. "Can I come to tea twice a week?"

"Sarah!" said Carole, and everyone laughed.

"You can come as often as you want!" said Wendy.

The expected phone call about Bella came from Joan Thompson the next morning. She was overjoyed to hear that Bella and her puppies were safe and would drive over from Middlesbrough straight away. She was desperate to see Bella again.

A large estate car drew up at the kennels shortly before six o'clock. Joan Thompson was close to tears as she got out of the car. Dressed in a green waxed jacket and jeans, she flicked loose strands of greying hair out of her eyes. Her face lit up when she saw Bella, who was waiting with Emily. The beagle tore across the yard towards her and leapt into her owner's arms.

Neil and Emily stood watching them together, feeling quite moved. Sam sat at their side. Neil ruffled the collie's ears. "What if we lost you, Sam?" He couldn't even bear to think of it.

Mrs Thompson turned to Bob Parker. "I don't know how to begin to thank you."

"Don't thank me," said Bob. "It's Neil and Emily who masterminded their great escape."

Mrs Thompson smiled at them. "I hardly know what to say. It's wonderful what you've done." She turned back to Bob. "I've brought the reward with me of course, but please let me know what I owe you for the kennels."

Bob shook his head. "That's all right, there were no kennel fees. Bella was kept in the rescue centre."

"Then please let me make a donation. It's the least I can do," said Mrs Thompson, as Carole Parker showed her into the office.

Carole returned a couple of minutes later with a broad grin on her face. "Hey, you two! There's something here you should see." She was holding up a cheque.

Emily stared at the amount and then handed it over to Neil. "Wow! It's enormous!"

Neil punched the air. "I think we'll be able to get that modem and scanner after all!" he said. "King Street Kennels will be on-line at last! World Wide Web here we come!"

Look out for Puppy Patrol No. 11:

Perfect Puppy

Is she too good to be true?

Lucky is King Street Kennels' newest visitor, and she looks like the perfect puppy. Her cheeky charm soon wins her heaps of friends – including little Sarah Parker.

But Lucky isn't as perfect as she looks – in fact, she's a seriously strange pup. And when she leaves King Street, Neil and Emily learn that this beautiful puppy is hiding a dangerous secret . . .

Puppy Patrol titles available from
Macmillan Children's Books

The prices shown below are correct at the time of
going to press. However, Macmillan Publishers
reserve the right to show new retail prices on covers
which may differ from those previously advertised.

1.	Teacher's Pet	Jenny Dale	£2.99
2.	Big Ben	Jenny Dale	£2.99
3.	Abandoned!	Jenny Dale	£2.99
4.	Double Trouble	Jenny Dale	£2.99
5.	Star Paws	Jenny Dale	£2.99
6.	Tug of Love	Jenny Dale	£2.99
7.	Saving Skye	Jenny Dale	£2.99
8.	Tugg's Luck	Jenny Dale	£2.99
9.	Red Alert	Jenny Dale	£2.99
10.	The Great Escape	Jenny Dale	£2.99

All Macmillan titles can be ordered at your local
bookshop or are available by post from:

Book Service by Post
PO Box 29, Douglas, Isle of Man IM99 1BQ

Credit cards accepted. For details:
Telephone: 01624 675137
Fax: 01624 670923
E-mail: bookshop@enterprise.net

Free postage and packing in the UK.